Baby Wombat's Week

written by
Jackie French

illustrated by
Bruce Whatley

Angus&Robertson
An imprint of HarperCollins*Publishers*

Angus&Robertson

An imprint of HarperCollins*Publishers*, Australia

First published in Australia in 2009
by HarperCollins*Publishers* Australia Pty Limited
ABN 36 009 913 517
www.harpercollins.com.au

HarperCollins*Publishers*

25 Ryde Road, Pymble, Sydney, NSW 2073, Australia
31 View Road, Glenfield, Auckland 0627, New Zealand
A53, Sector 57, Noida, UP, India
77–85 Fulham Palace Road, London W6 8JB, United Kingdom
2 Bloor Street East, 20th Floor, Toronto, Ontario M4W 1AA, Canada
10 East 53rd Street, New York NY 10032, USA

National Library of Australia Cataloguing-in-Publication data:

French, Jackie.
   Baby wombat's week / Jackie French ; illustrator: Bruce Whatley.
   ISBN: 9780732286941 (hbk.)
   ISBN: 9780732286958 (pbk.)
   For children.
   Wombats—Juvenile fiction.
   Whatley, Bruce.
A823.3

Bruce Whatley used acrylic paints on watercolour paper to create the illustrations for this book
Original cover and internal design by Matt Stanton; based on design by HarperCollins Design Studio
Colour reproduction by Graphic Print Group, Adelaide, South Australia
Printed in China at Phoenix Offset, on 128gsm Matt Art

7 6 5 4 3 2 1   09 10 11 12

To Lisa, who has crafted the journey of Bruce, Mothball and me
from the beginning, and added endless magic.
PS *And to Noël, Jennifer, Bounce and Burper too, with much love.*
JF

For Sylvia Rose
BW

Monday

Early morning: slept.

Slept.

Late morning: slept.

BORED...

Bou^nced.

Mum decided
It was time to PLAY...

OUTSIDE!

Smelled the flowers.

Ate the flowers.

Flowers are

YUMMMMM...

Another smell...?

It smells like me!

Here it is!

Played with my friend.

I won!

Tuesday

Early morning: slept.

Slept.

Late morning: played.

I'm
HUNGRY!

(Human food is weird ...)

Afternoon: slept.

Wednesday

Morning: woke up.

BORED...

Mum says we need a new hole. A BIGGER one!

Dug a new hole for all of us.

Afternoon: Scratched.

A lot.

Thursday

Morning: Mum says new hole is too small.

Afternoon: Hunted for **another** new hole.

Will we ever find a hole BIG enough for Mum and me?

Friday

Morning:

Found a GIANT hole!

Afternoon:

Told Mum about hole!

Mum said, 'Go to sleep.'

NOT... tired...

Saturday

Morning:

Who stole our hole?

Mum says never mind.

We'll dig the BEST hole EVER!

I wonder
what we'll find up here?

We've found a hole!

The most ENORMOUS hole!

A hole for me ... and my mum.

Sunday

Morning: slept.